I0561668

E. Rothesay Miller

Princess Splendor

The wood-cutter's daughter

E. Rothesay Miller

Princess Splendor
The wood-cutter's daughter

ISBN/EAN: 9783337165031

Printed in Europe, USA, Canada, Australia, Japan

Cover: Foto ©Andreas Hilbeck / pixelio.de

More available books at **www.hansebooks.com**

Japanese Fairy Tale Series, Extra No.

Princess Splendor

The Wood-cutter's Daughter.

Translated into English by E. Rothesay Miller.

TOKYO:

Published by the Kobunsha,

8, Maruyacho.

1889.

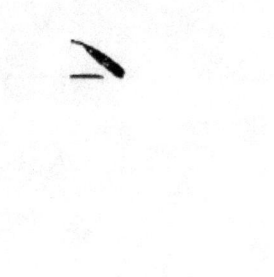

Contents.

PRINCESS SPLENDOR

THE WOOD-CUTTER'S DAUGHTER.

Once upon a time long, long ago there was an old wood-cutter called Taketori who lived all alone with his wife in a little cottage at the foot of a mountain. He was so poor that he made his living by wandering o'er hill and dale cutting bamboos and bringing them home to be made into all sorts of useful things.

One day in returning home, while passing through a grove, he saw what seemed to be a soft light shining from near the roots

of one of the bamboos, on going close to it he
found that the light came from a tiny fairy
no longer than his hand, who was shut

up in the stem of the bamboo. Wondering greatly he took the little fairy, who glowed like a beautiful fire-fly, home to his wife saying, that surely it

must be for them because he had found it among his old friends the bamboos.

In three short months the tiny fairy grew into a gentle girl and then to a fair and noble woman, and her foster parents decided that it was time to give her a name and have her dressed and treated as became her grace and beauty. This, the old bamboo-cutter was able to do, for ever since the day he first saw her in the wood, whenever he cut down a bamboo, he found gold concealed between the joints; and thus little by little he grew richer and richer till finally he built a magnificent house and kept a retinue of servants. Now although their daughter had grown so beautiful, that there was no one in the whole world with whom she could be compared, she was just as gentle as she was beautiful, the joy of her

parents' hearts and the light of their home, for the same soft radiance ever shone from her wherever she went and there was no need of lamp or candle in her presence.

When the time came for naming her, a royal feast was given, to which the guests from all the country round were invited. The name selected for her was Nayo Take no Kaguya Hime, Princess Splendor of the Feathery Bamboo, as expressive of her lithe figure and supernatural radiance. During the three days of the feast any one might look unabashed upon the bewildering beauty of the princess, but after the festivities were over her parents kept her within the inner rooms and gardens of the palace, so that not even those who lived near by could get a glimpse of her fair face.

THE COURTING.

It was not long before the fame of the princess' beauty spread far and wide, till there was not a man in all the world who was not crazy to see her. Even many of the nobility left their palaces and spent day and night hovering around the garden enclosure, hoping that by some happy chance they might get a passing sight of her through an opening in the hedge-row.

Among the many suitors who came to court the beautiful princess were two princes of the blood royal and three of the highest nobles in the realm, who by their rank and persevering devotion commended themselves to the old bamboo-cutter. But

he was unwilling to compel his daughter to wed against her will, and as she refused their suit, he advised them to return to their palaces and forget all about the wood-cutter's daughter. They tried to follow his advice but found it impossible to blot the fair image from their hearts, so, finally, comforting themselves with the thought that she must in the end wed some one, back they came through storm and sunshine, heat and cold, hovering near the palace gardens like moths around a fire that will surely scorch their wings.

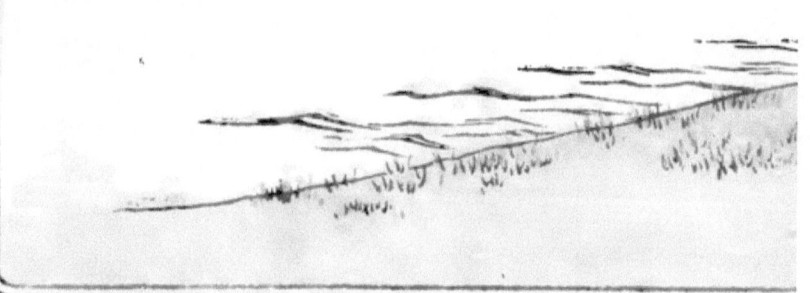

The old wood-cutter seeing their constancy endeavored to persuade his daughter to change her mind, saying, "Ah dear daughter, though I know quite well that you are a real fairy,—and it may be that fairies never wed, —yet we have brought you up and loved you as if you were our very own daughter, and now that you have grown into a beautiful woman we must treat you like a woman and provide a husband for you ; for although you might be very happy here as long as I am alive, still I am now over seventy, and who can tell but that I may die tomorrow, so I beg you to consider well and choose from among these distinguished nobles one who can be your husband and protect you after I am gone."

The princess laughingly replied, that fairy or no fairy, she loved dear old Taketori as if

he were her own father and was only too
ready to do all that he wished, but,—men
were so fickle! and,—she was afraid these
great nobles did not realize that she was
brought up as a poor wood-cutter's child and
they might tire of her very soon ;—and so,—·
she would like them to do some great thing
to shew that they were really as devoted to
her as they professed to be.

To this they all agreed; but the pretty
princess, hoping to get rid of all her suitors
at once and forever, sent one of them to India
to find the stone bowl of Buddha; another
to seek in the Eastern Ocean a mountain
called Hōrai and bring a branch of a tree
which grew there with silver roots, golden
trunk and jewels for fruit; a third was to go
to China and get a fur robe made of the skins

of fire-rats; a fourth was to bring her the rainbow-jewel from the dragon's neck; and the last was to find the shell which the swallows keep hidden away in their nests.

Sad indeed were the hearts of these nobles as they went away, for it was now plain to them that the princess wished never to see them again.

THE

STONE BOWL OF BUDDHA.

The prince who was to go to India to get
the stone bowl of Buddha was a lazy man,
and though he wished so very much to marry
the princess, yet he thought he would
never reach India alive if he had to cross
all those hundreds and thousands of miles
of sea, and even if he got there, how was
he to know where to look for the bowl. However, he sent word to the princess that he
had set out for India that very day,
but he really went away and
concealed himself for three years,
the time it would take to go to India
and come back again. At the end of
the three years he went quietly to a little

temple, hidden away up in the mountains, and there in front of the shrine, he found an old stone bowl covered with soot and dirt; taking this he put it in a bag of beautiful silk brocade, and fastening to it a branch of artificial flowers, he dropped a letter in the bowl telling how he had shed his heart's blood in crossing seas and mountains to obtain it, and then sent the gift to the princess.

The princess was greatly astonished to see the bowl, for she did not think this lazy prince would take the trouble to go to India, but she had not yet proved it. She knew, that if it were the real bowl of Buddha it ought to sparkle like diamonds, and so hastening to open the bag she looked inside. There was nothing there but the letter, so she sent the gift back to the prince, who, however,

instead of being ashamed of having his trick discovered, wrote a pretty little poem to the princess, in which he said, that indeed the bowl had sparkled, but as soon as *she* looked on it the light died out, dimmed by the brightness of her eyes, and though he threw away the bowl he threw away at the same time all shame and still begged for her favor.

To this the princess did not deign an answer; but from that time till this, when any one has thrown away all sense of shame* and does what he ought not he is said to have " thrown away the bowl**."

* Haji.　　** Hachi.

THE JEWEL BRANCH
OF HŌRAI.

Now the prince who was sent in quest
of the floating mountain of Hōrai was very
cunning and very rich, and he determined
to spare neither treasure nor pains in
gaining the hand of Princess Splendor.
To the court nobles he pretended that
he was going to some celebrated hot-
springs for his health and would not be
back for a long time, but to the princess
he sent word that he was about
to set out in quest of the jewel-
branch. A numerous band of
retainers accompanied him to
the sea shore, where he dismissed
them, saying that he wished

to travel quietly and would take only a few personal attendants; with these he embarked and sailed away towards the west.

That was the last the princess heard of him for three years ; but one day there came a rumor to the palace, that the prince had returned from his travels bringing a branch of the wonderful Udon flower which blooms but once in three thousand years. Before she had time to recover from her surprise at this news, her maids brought in a richly ornamented box containing, what seemed to be, a branch of some unknown tree covered with rare, sweet blossoms. On looking closer, however, she saw that this was no real tree, for the bark was of ruddy gold, the leaves of silver, and the flowers shining jewels of many tints ; and fastened by a silken thread was a

letter in which the prince declared, that though he was willing to risk his life in meeting unknown dangers, he had resolved never to return till he had plucked "The Jewel-Branch,"—meaning Lady Splendor herself. The princess admired the glittering jewels, as she held them in her hands, but sighed to think that just because her wishes had been so faithfully fulfilled she would have to wed the prince. Just then old Taketori entered and announced the prince, all travel stained from his long journey, come to claim the fulfilment of her promise. The princess answered nothing, but leaning a sad face upon her hand seemed lost in revery. The old wood-cutter could not understand his daughter's reluctance to wed so rich and handsome a suitor who had proved his devotion by such a marvellous gift, but all his urging only brought the response, that she had asked her suitors to do what she had fondly hoped would prove impossible, lest he should think her unfilial in refusing his request to choose a husband.

Old Taketori hereupon went out to the prince and begged him to tell of his journey, as he was sure there must be marvellous adventures connected with the finding of such jewels. The prince nothing loath began: —" It was more than two years ago, when on the tenth day of the second moon I set out on my travels, fully resolved never to return without the Jewel-Branch of Hōrai. I knew not where to go, but trusting to fair fortune, spread my sail to the first breeze that blew. It was not long before fierce storms

arose and the waves seemed ready to swallow
us, as we looked shuddering down into the
very bottom of the sea ; at other times, we
lay becalmed, our food all gone, and we
barely able to eke out our lives on the poor
shell-fish found on barren shores; sometimes,
smitten with loathsome disease we writhed
in agony, the very heavens shutting us out
from all mercy ; often, horrible demons rising from the waves climbed with slimy coil
upon the ship, ready to devour us. On the
five hundredth day, while drifting on an
unknown sea, at the hour of the dragon, I
saw, far off upon the horizon, a hugh mass
which proved to be a beautiful floating
mountain. We approached and sailed around
it for three days, trying to find a place to
land, at last, when drawing close to the shore

in a sheltered cove, I saw a woman catching the limpid water from a tiny rill in her silver bucket, who was so surpassingly beautiful in her glistening robes, that I thought she surely must be an angel. When, in reply to my eager question, she told me the mountain was called Hōrai, I could scarce restrain my joy to ask her own name; she murmured some softly musical word and vanished, and I never saw her more.

"All around were shrubs and trees laden with flowers such as bloom only in the stars, the streams which broke in laughing cascades of diamonds over the glittering rocks were of red-gold, pure silver, or bright azure waters, and were spanned with fairy bridges of precious stones of all the colors of the rainbow. Among the trees which sparkled

in the sun-light, I saw the very one the princess had described, from which I plucked this branch, although there were many others more beautiful and more wonderful. In such a fairy land one could well wish to remain forever, but the moment I had obtained the branch my heart beat to return, so hastening to the ship, with fair winds, we arrived within four hundred days and waiting not to change my robes all wet with the salt sea spray here I am come."

Old Taketori was so affected by the story of the prince's woes that he could hardly keep back the tears, but just then, six men entered the garden bearing a letter held in a split stick. One of them came near and, making a profound bow, begged that they might receive the payment for working a thousand days on the jewel-branch. The old man could not speak for astonishment and, on looking towards the prince, saw him pale and trembling not daring to meet his eye. As the rooms of the princess opened on the garden, she had seen the men enter and, overhearing something of what they said, sent one of her women to summon them before her.

Their story was soon told. It appeared that the prince, who had just given such a pathetic tale of his voyage, had in reality returned in three days after setting sail, but very secretly, and went to a house he had prepared with three thick walls so that no prying eye might know what was going on within. Here he had lived for three years with six skilful workmen, to whom he had

promised rich rewards, as well as official rank, if they would make a branch just like the one the princess ordered. This they had done, but receiving neither rank nor wages, they had made bold to come to the palace of the princess, since they had heard that she was soon to wed this prince and had received the jewel-branch as a marriage gift.

The princess, whose heart had been sinking with the declining sun, now sprang up all smiles and clapping her little hands ordered the men to be well paid for their good news, then hastily replacing the jewels in their case ; she gave them to the old wood-cutter, who, going to the prince, so pitied his mortification, that without a word he placed it by his side and withdrew. The poor prince could neither sit nor stand but lay crouching on the porch, from which he would not move till the sun set, when he stole away into the darkness.

The workmen, rejoicing in their good fortune, were returning to their homes, when they were attacked by the miserable prince smarting with shame, who, snatching away the money bestowed by the princess, trampled it in the dust and beat them most unmercifully, till they were glad to escape with their lives.

As for the prince he did not dare to return to his palace, for he knew that every one would hear of his disgrace, which he could never hope to outlive, so he fled to the mountains and would not let even his friends know where he was; and though search was made far and near he has never been heard of to this day.

THE FIRE ROBE.

Lord Abé, whom the princess had ordered
to go to China to get her the fire-robe, was
very rich and much respected and had friends
in all parts of the land. One of these
lived over in China, and to him he
despatched a faithful retainer with a
large sum of money and begged him to
spare neither time nor trouble in procuring
a fur dress made of the skins of fire-rats,
—whatever they might be. The friend read
the letter and exclaimed, " Well, well!
here's a pretty to-do! To be sure
I have heard of fire-rats, but a robe
of their skins is not to be had for the
asking, indeed it is only once in a lifetime

that one is brought from India. If it were for any one but Lord Abé I would positively decline to have anything to do with it, but for him I shall do my very best, though I am sure I do not know how to set about it."

After long and careful inquiry he learned that years before a holy hermit from India had brought a mantle, or dress of some kind, made of the skins of fire-rats, but what had become of it,—that, nobody knew. One day by mere chance he learned that this fur robe was carefully kept as a sacred relic in a temple away off in the western mountains.

To this temple he despatched a messenger carrying letters of recommendation from high officials. By the help of these letters he at last obtained the robe, but had to pay

more money for it than even Lord Abé had sent.

The servant of his lordship, bearing the precious parcel, hastened home from China and landing at the nearest port he mounted a swift horse, sent by his master to meet him, and rode the whole distance to the capital, four hundred miles, in seven days.

His lordship was so delighted to get the fur robe that he did not give a second thought to the money expended, but turning his face towards China, fell on his knees and worshipped. Then, picturing to himself how queenly Princess Splendor would look with this rich garment clinging to her graceful form, he replaced it in the exquisite box encrusted with jewels and hastened away to the palace with his treasure.

The princess expressed her admiration, when her women shook from its folds the rich golden-green fur which shimmered like silver in the sun-light, and though she admitted that it looked as if it were real, yet since her other lovers had tried to deceive her, she determined to put this one to the test, and knowing, that if the robe were genuine it could not be burnt, she requested Lord Abé to put it in the fire.

The old wood-cutter protested against this, as he was displeased with his daughter for rejecting the two princes, and was afraid that she might treat this suitor in the same way. Her foster-mother, too, had long been anxious that her daughter should wed, and now that her husband had asked the nobleman into the house, rejoiced to think that the marriage

was so soon to take place. Since the princess insisted, Lord Abé consented to have the dress put into the fire, but he could not understand why she should doubt its genuineness, because he had taken so much trouble to obtain it.

When he saw the beautiful robe crackling
in the flames and his bright hopes turning
to ashes with it, his heart sank and his
cheeks paled, for he, too, had been deceived;
and he sadly turned his steps homeward
with the poor consolation, that
the princess pitied him;
for she wrote, that had
she known the
fur would
burn

she would
not
have
put it in the fire.

THE DRAGON JEWEL.

Lord Lofty, though a great boaster, was also a great coward and, to escape any danger that might befall himself, he called together all his retainers and told them that whoever brought him the rainbow-jewel, from off the dragon's neck, should have whatever he asked. The men replied, that it was bad enough to be expected to get any kind of jewel, but utterly impossible to obtain one from the neck of a dragon. Hearing this the pompous lord exclaimed. that *he* had always supposed that vassals were bound to obey their lord even if they lost their lives in doing so; and anyhow he

did not see why they made so much fuss about it, for he had not told them to go to some far away country, like China or India, since dragons could be found anywhere rising out of the sea and floating on clouds up and down the mountains.

The men seeing what a temper he was in, said, very well, they were ready to obey his commands no matter what they were. Whereupon their lord smiling praised them for their fidelity and bidding them not to shew their faces again till they brought the dragon-jewel, opened his storehouses and took out all the silk, cotton, gold, and copper to serve as expenses for their travels and sent them away.

Since they had been commanded not to shew their faces without the dragon-jewel,

which they knew they could not obtain, they
laughed at their lord for his foolish whim and,
dividing the treasures up among them, set
out in any direction to which their feet happened to point, each one spending his time
to suit his own fancy. Some returned secretly to their homes and lived with their
families, others spent their lord's money in
drinking and pleasure, but none of them
returned to the palace.

Lord Lofty thinking that it would never
do to let the Princess Splendor live in a com-
mon house, had a gorgeous palace built, with
stained and lacquered woods, the roof thatched with silken threads, and the inside adorn-
ed with striped damask and all kinds of rich
woven hangings. Then, being so very sure
of obtaining the princess, he dismissed all

the ladies of his palace and waited impa-
tiently the return of his vassals with the dragon-jewel.   But after waiting a whole year,
his patience was exhausted and, taking only
two trusty attendants, he went to the nearest
sea-port and inquired, if the retainers of the
great Lord Lofty had not yet returned from
killing the dragon and capturing the jewel on
its neck. The sailors laughed loudly and
said, that this was more easily said than done.
Thereupon the lord flourished his bow and
arrows and declared, that if there were such
a thing in this world as a dragon, he would
kill it dead with his great strong bow and
then shew them who could take the jewel
from its neck. Saying which he embarked
on one of the ships and set sail for the west.

Every thing went smoothly for some days

but gradually the wind grew stronger, the waves dashed higher, the lightning flashed, and the thunder-bolts seemed ready to fall on them. Lord Lofty was frightened out of his wits and the pilot with streaming eyes said, that he had sailed in many ships before but had never been in such a pitiable plight as this, for if they were not overwhelmed by the waves they would certainly be struck by the thunder-bolts, and even should they be saved from the lightning they would be driven into the South Sea and miserably perish. Hearing this Lord Lofty lost what little heart he had left and growing deathly sea-sick he sobbed out, that he always thought, the pilot was the hope of the ship and he did not see why he should frighten him so.

The pilot replied, that it was all very well

to blame him, and if he were a god he would
gladly do what was wanted, but the real reason why the wind blew and the waves rose
and the thunder was about to fall on them
was, that he had said he intended to kill the
dragon, and this storm was of the dragon's
raising, and so he had better pray with all his
might. The poor noble fell on his knees and
between his tears kept saying over and over
a thousand times, "Oh, dear me! I said I
would kill a dragon, but I never, never will
touch the tip of a single hair, if you only
let me off this time." Pretty soon the thunder ceased and it grew a little lighter, but the
wind still blew strong, and although the pilot
assured his cowardly master that the wind
was fair, he would not believe it.

The wind continued blowing for several

days and at last they came to land and found that they were in the country of Harima on the Inland Sea, but the poor frightened nobleman thought they were drifting in the South Sea and lay trembling in the bottom of the boat. It was only when the governor of the province came and had him lifted out on a mat and placed under the trees that he began to realize that he was actually on dry land once more. He had caught a heavy cold and both his eyes were so swollen that they looked as if plums were fastened beneath them, while he shook all over from the effects of the sea-sickness and fright, and altogether he was so supremely ridiculous that no one could keep from laughing at him.

Having once landed nothing could induce him to go on the ship again, so they procured

a palanquin and putting him in carried him like a great pig, groaning and grunting every step of the way home.

When his retainers, who had been sent in search of the dragon-jewel, heard in what a plight their lord had returned, they plucked up courage and came before him; and he, instead of blaming them, praised them for the wisdom they had shewn in not attempting to do what was impossible, and the little money he had left he divided among them, calling the Princess Splendor all sorts of dreadful names, saying she was no better than a murderess for trying to make away with good men's lives, and advised his people never to pass her house again.

The story got out that Lord Lofty had come back with the dragon-jewel, but those who knew better laughed till they nearly split their sides, saying, that the only jewels he brought were the plum-jewels under each eye. And from this, when any one has not been able to do as he boasted he would, he is said to have "brought home the plum-jewels."

The gorgeous palace built for his marriage with the princess was never used, and the crows came and built their nests of the silken threads with which it was thatched.

THE SHELL
IN THE SWALLOW'S NEST.

Lord Overstone, after receiving the commands of the princess, sent for the chief of his retainers and asked him if he knew where a swallow was building its nest. The chief, much surprised, inquired what his lord wanted to do with a swallow's nest; and when he heard, it was not the nest but the little cowry-shell which the swallow keeps hidden away, that he wanted, he replied, that he did not know about the *shells,* but he had killed many swallows and had never found anything in their stomachs worth having, but possibly these shells were to be found when they laid their eggs;

however, as there were a great many swallows building nests in the thatch of the kitchen of a nobleman's house not far away, in the holes through which the smoke escaped, if some one climbed up to the roof, he could soon see if there were any cowry-shells in the nests when they laid their eggs.

The lord highly delighted immediately sent twenty men down to the kitchen, where they built a scaffolding and climbed to the roof. They had scarcely reached the roof, when their master sent to know if they had not found the cowry-shell. But the swallows were so frightened by the confusion that they had flown far away and would not come back to their nests.

The lord was at his wit's end, when an old retainer came up and whispering in his ear

told him that they had set about the matter in an absurd way, for the swallow being a timorous bird could not be induced to lay eggs as long as so many menwere about. He advised him to take all the scaffolding down and have a strong basket prepared, so that at the right minute some one could be raised up to the nests. He had heard that swallows always flirted their tails and turned round and round seven times before laying their eggs, and he thought that if at that time some one slipped in his hand carefully he would find the cowry-shell.

His lordship much pleased ordered the scaffolding to be taken down and spent the evening feasting with his retainers, and when he went home he took off his handsome coat and gave it, as a special mark of favor, to the old man who was to take charge of the work on the morrow.

Towards evening the next day, Lord Overstone hastened off to the kitchen to see if they had found one of the cowry-shells; but to his great disappointment, the man who had been hoisted up to the nests had found nothing. The lord petulently exclaimed, that it was because he had not searched carefully enough, and insisting upon getting into the basket himself, he told the men to haul it up; reaching the nest just in time, he saw the swallow turning round and round, and so, slipping his hand quietly into the nest, he touched something smooth and cold, which he grasped tightly and calling out, "Lower away old man, I have found it," they began to lower the basket; but the rope, which by this

time was much worn, suddenly broke and he fell backwards on the top of an iron caldron. The men sprang forward very much frightened and lifting the apparently dying lord off the lid of the caldron placed him carefully on the ground and moistened his lips with some water. He slowly opened his eyes and, motioning for a candle to be brought, whispered, that he wished to see the shell which would gain the princess but had cost him so dear. Opening his hand, there was no shell, nothing but a little piece of dirt, which he dropped and sank back exhausted.

Borne to his palace, his one thought was to hide his disgrace from everybody, for he would rather die of his wounds than live to be laughed at, and the very thought of people making fun of him made him worse.

The princess hearing of his accident sent to inquire after his health, saying in a little couplet, that she wished to know whether it were true, that, after all these years of waiting, his labor had been in vain and he had not obtained the shell.

When Lord Overstone received the letter he was very weak, but getting some one to hold the paper, with great difficulty, he wrote, that it was reward enough to have the princess pity him, even though she could not save his life already passing away; and falling back he expired.

THE
ROYAL HUNTING PARTY.

In the course of time, the fame of the Princess Splendor's beauty and the sad fate of all her wooers reached the imperial court and the Mikado himself became possessed with a desire to see this bewitching coquette; so he sent the Lady Tassel to the house of the old wood-cutter to bring him word just what kind of a person she was.

This noble lady proceeded in grand state to the house of the princess and, being met by the wood-cutter's wife, haughtily said, that she had come by His Majesty's express command to see the princess. Her old

foster-mother tried to persuade the princess
to meet this grand lady, but she positively
declined and said that, really, she did not
see, why she need trouble herself so much
about the commands of the Mikado. The
old woman was dreadfully shocked at this
disrespectful reply, but, as there was no
help for it, she went out to Lady Tassel
and tried to excuse her daughter by saying,
that she was such a child she was entirely
too bashful to meet Her Excellency. Lady
Tassel did not take the matter so compla-
cently, however, and angrily said, it was
impossible for her to return to the palace
without seeing the princess; besides whoever heard of such a thing, as any one
daring to disobey the commands of the
King. When her mother reported these

words to the princess, her bright eyes flashed and she replied with spirit, "Indeed! since then I have broken the commands of this high and mighty king, let him kill me if he likes, I never *will* meet that woman."

So the Lady Tassel had to return with her grand retinue, with what dignity she could, and report to the Mikado the failure of her errand. The Mikado laughed out, "O! the little flirt! she wants to break my heart too, as she has broken the hearts of all her other wooers"; and he tried to think no more about it. But the more he tried the less he could forget, and so he settled the matter by sending for Taketori and asking his daughter in marriage. The old man came trembling into the presence of the emperor and kneeling said, that he had been greatly distressed by the way his daughter had treated His Majesty's messenger and he would return and make known His August wishes. The Mikado, to place the matter beyond all dispute, said, that surely Taketori had a right to dispose of his own daughter's hand as he pleased, and if the marriage were consummated he would bestow a high rank on the old wood-cutter.

Taketori highly delighted went home and urged the princess to comply with the wishes of the Mikado: but she declared, that she never, never would be a palace slave, and if her father insisted upon it, through his desire for rank and office, she would just vanish and they would never see her any more. "What are rank and office," ex-

claimed the old man excitedly, "if I lose my child :—but really now," he continued, secretly longing for the grandeur promised, "what danger is there of your fading into nothing; had you no better try life at the palace after all"? The princess said sadly, "If you wish I will try, but I *know* that I shall die." "No, no," said her father, "I will go and tell the Mikado, that you can not comply with his wishes"; and hastened to the palace.

The Mikado did not believe in the princess' fading away any more than Taketori did, but after thinking for a while told him, that he would go out with a hunting party and when near Taketori's house, at the foot of the mountain, would come in and take the princess by surprise, before she had time to refuse

to see him. This plan pleased the old man; and before many days the Mikado gave orders for a hunting party and set out for the mountains. On reaching the house of Take-tori, he suddenly entered, without being announced, and saw, that it was filled with a soft radiance, and there,—sure enough,—was the most entrancingly lovely being he had ever seen, even in his dreams. Knowing that this must be the princess, he caught her by her flowing sleeve as she fled into the inner room; she turned away her head and hid her face in her other sleeve, but not until he had caught one glimpse of a face so purely lovely that it would haunt him for evermore. The Mikado declared that he would not let her go, she must return with him to the palace, but the princess replied, that as she was not an earth-born maiden, it was impossible to comply with his wishes; whereupon the Mikado threw his arm around her waist, intending to carry her off bodily, when,—wonderful to relate,—she faded away from his sight; and he was convinced, that she was no human being but only a beautiful fairy. He begged her to come back that he might see her once more before returning to the palace, and the princess appeared again, filling the room with rosy light. Taking a long farewell look he went out, bitterly disappointed that the princess was lost to him, but yet so glad that she had not vanished forever from the earth, that he knighted old Taketori on the spot and gave him command of the one hundred men who accompanied him.

Sadly the Mikado returned to the now

desolate palace, for he knew that no woman in all the court was worthy to be compared with the princess. Hereafter whenever a celebrated beauty was presented at court she seemed, to the Mikado, not worth looking at, as he remembered that glorious face which he had seen but once. He spent his years alone, his only pleasure was sending to the princess letters or poems fastened to rare plants and receiving her replies. In this way the Mikado spent three happy years.

THE
HEAVENLY FEATHER DRESS.

As time passed on, at the return of each full-moon the princess seemed sad and depressed and would steal away by herself upon the balcony and weeping gaze at the moon.

Taketori being told of this went to her room and said, "Ah! my dear little fairy! what is it that troubles you so in this bright and beautiful world? Do not look at the moon if it makes you sad." So the princess tried hard to hide her sorrow, but when mid-summer came she could no longer conceal her grief but wept day and night. Her parents insisting upon

knowing what was
the matter, she sobbed out,
"From the very beginning of
spring, have I wished to tell you, but was
afraid of distressing you too much, and now
I *must* speak. I am really a child of the

moon and in the bright capital there have
a father and mother.   Compelled
by a decree of fate,
I came to this earth for a while,
but now the time approaches
when I must return, and
at the full-moon of

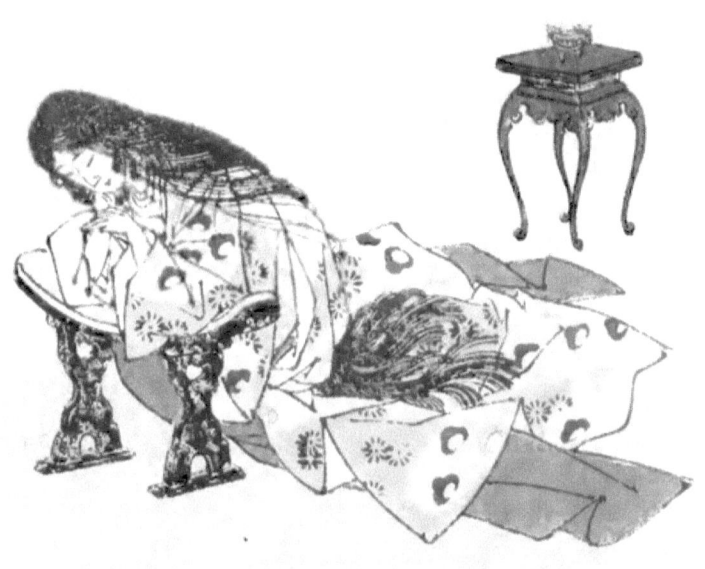

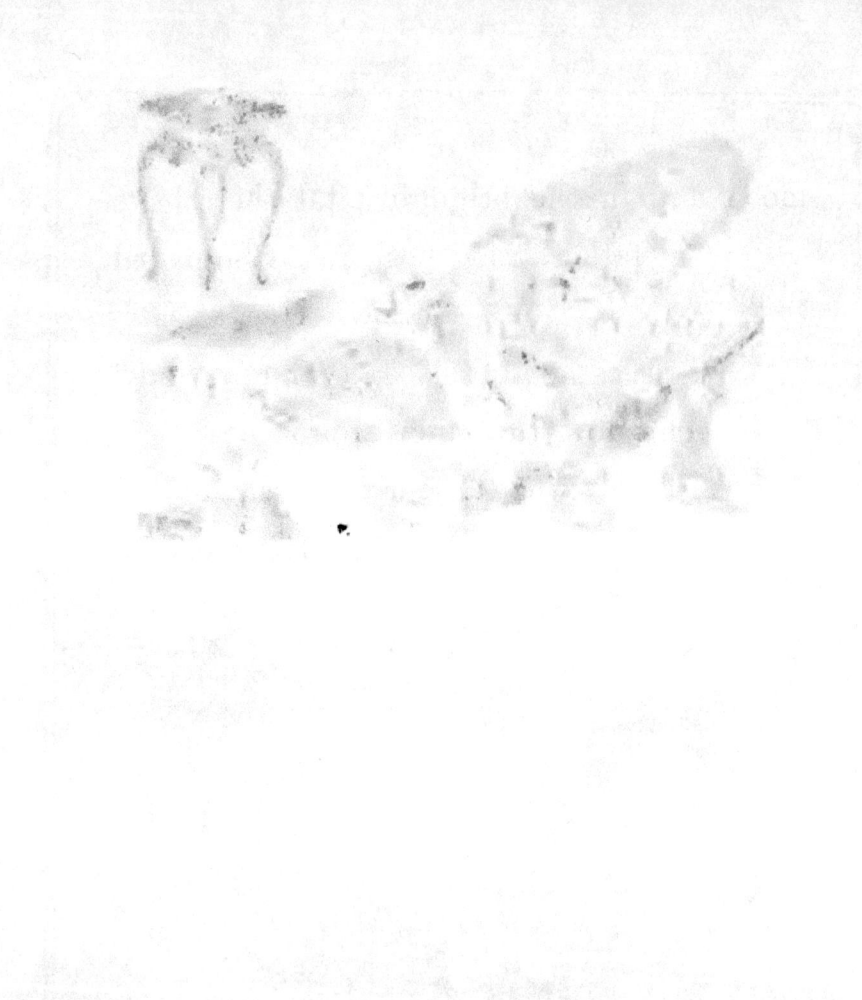

this month, some one will come to take me back. Do not think that I wish to leave you and go to my former home!" she exclaimed, as the old wood-cutter unable to control himself burst into a violent flood of tears, crying, " Ah! what are you saying? When I found you among the bamboos you were no bigger than a rape-seed, and look! now you are as tall as I am. Do you think I will let anybody from the moon carry off my little fairy ? "

Her attendants too, who had been brought up with her and knew her lovely disposition, could not bear the thought of parting from their gentle mistress. And they all wept together.

The Mikado hearing of this strange story, sent a messenger to Taketori to ask if the report were true. Taketori told the reason of their sorrow and begged that the Mikado would, at the time of the full-moon, send a strong guard to keep the princess from being carried off.

The messenger reported to His Majesty what he had heard, and said that Taketori, who, he supposed, was only fifty years old, looked at least a hundred, he was so bowed down with anxiety and grief. The Mikado gave orders, that one of his skilful generals, together with the commanders of the six divisions of the army, should take two thousand soldiers and guard the house.

One thousand men were ranged upon the ramparts and one thousand on the roof of the house. The ladies also of the princess' apartments took their long spears and stood

guard in the corridors, while in the inner treasure-house her foster-mother sat holding the princess in her arms and old Taketori remained on guard at the door.

When all was ready the old man declared that even an angel could not enter the house, and boastingly told the men on the roof to shoot with their arrows whatever came from the sky, even though it were but a dew-drop. The princess, however, warned him that all his preparations were useless, because no human being could fight the inhabitants of the moon, and no matter how closely she was shut in, everything would open of its own accord as soon as *they* appeared.

The old man angrily declared that he would tear their eyes out with his long nails, pull their hair out by the roots, and stripping them of their clothes drive them away naked and ashamed.

The princess tried to stop his loud boasting and went on to say, how sorry she was that she had to go now before she had been long enough with her parents to repay even a small part of all their care, and how she had hoped to watch over them when they were old and feeble; and though for some time she had been begging her parents in the moon to let her stay just one year more, they would not permit it. But she had no wish to return to that land, although the people there never grew old or died or had any sorrow. Her old father tried to comfort her, by saying that he would not let one of the moon-men touch her, no matter how grand or how powerful he might be.

The night wore on
as they were
talking

together,
when at midnight,
suddenly, all
around the palace grew bright as
day, just

as if ten full-moons.
were shining ; while from the sky
descended a great
company of men clad in the

most gorgeous raiment, who ranged
themselves in the air

about five feet from the
ground.

The guards
of the palace seemed
to be in a night-mare they were

so frightened, and when they tried to draw
their bows, their fingers had no power and
their arms hung by their sides. Even
those, who by an effort of will, forced
themselves to shoot their arrows, missed
their aim and with the rest stood and stared
like idiots.

One among the host seemed like a king,
so splendidly did his garments glitter in the
moonlight; he approached Taketori and began to speak, but the poor old man, who so
short a time before had been boasting what
he would do, now seemed like a drunken
man and fell forward on his face. "Young
Gray-beard," said the moon-man, "the
Princess Splendor, for having committed
some great sin, was banished from the courts
of the moon and forced to live on earth; and

as a reward for your honesty and goodness she was sent to your miserable hovel for a short time and, at the same time, you were given gold enough to make you rich; but now, the time of her punishment having expired, we have come to take her back. Quickly bring her forth."

The people in the moon, since they never die or grow old, thought Taketori very young in spite of his gray hairs; and to them an earthly palace seemed miserable and dirty, when compared with the glittering palaces of the moon.

The old man thinking to put them off replied, " The Princess Splendor has lived with us for twenty years, and since you say the one you are looking for has been away from the moon for only a *short* time, there may

be another Princess Splendor for all I know ; anyhow, the Princess Splendor who lives here is dangerously ill and can not possibly come out."

To this the kingly leader did not deign to reply, but ordered the flying-chariot to be made ready and the gauze umbrella, which they had brought with them, to be spread over it, and then calling to the princess said, "Come, come how can you remain so long in this dirty place."

At these words the outer doors, which had been so securely fastened, flew open and the inner panels slid aside of their own accord, and the princess, who was held so tightly, came forth, for her mother's arms dropped powerless, and she could only look and weep.

The princess turned to Taketori who

seemed completely dazed and asked if he would not bid her good-bye. "How can I bid you good-bye, for what is to become of me after you go? Oh! do not leave me behind, take me with you!" he sobbed.

As Taketori was so overcome with grief that he could not recollect anything, the princess said she would write a letter which he could read after she was gone. In the letter she said, if she were an earthly maiden, it would be her greatest pleasure to watch over and tenderly care for him till he passed away. But now, as that could not be, she would leave her dress with him as a memento, and if, when the moon was full, he would gaze on it and think of her and read her letter, she would be watching him from the moon and he might think the soft moon-

beams were her hands smoothing the wrinkles from his brow.

One of the moon-men offered the princess a medicine called the Elixir of Life, to purify her body from all earthly taint, this she tasted and folded some in the garment which she was to leave with Taketori. Another bright angel was about to wrap her in a mantle curiously wrought of brilliant feathers, when the princess exclaimed, "Wait a little! one who wears this garment breaks all earthly ties and I have yet one other duty to fulfil;" then, slowly, before them all, she began to write the following lines to the Mikado:

"Although Your Majesty has been pleased to send this great host to prevent my leaving this earth, yet I may not stay. I truly grieve for Your Majesty's disappointment, for though I have been so rude as not to comply with Your August wishes, yet has Your Majesty deigned to keep me in Your Royal thoughts:" closing with these lines, "My latest thought on leaving earth, ere taking flight for heaven—has been of Thee." This she sent to the Mikado with the vial of the elixir.

Having thus bade farewell to earth, wrapped in the shining mantle,—old Taketori's grief and all her own sorrow forgotten,— mounting the chariot, accompanied by hundreds of warriors from the moon, the Princess Splendor rose towards the skies and vanished into the bright moonlight.

After the princess had gone her foster-parents, plunged in grief, wandered through

the house bewildered. Though they listened to the letter of the princess, when it was read to them, they did not realize its contents and lost all interest in life, moaning, that they had no one to live for, nothing to do in the world, and refusing to taste the deathless medicine they took to their beds never to rise again.

The general returned with the soldiers to the royal palace and told minutely all that had happened and how unsuccessful they had been in trying to detain the princess. When the Mikado received the vial and read the letter, he was overwhelmed with grief and refused to eat or to allow the musicians to amuse him, but calling an officer he bade him seek out the highest mountain in the land, one that was nearest heaven, ascending which he was to kindle a fire on the topmost

peak and burn both the vial
and a poem, in which he had
written :

> "Even the memory of our one
> meeting floats in tears,
> Why then should I wish the
> deathless draught ?"

The officer, appointed to carry out the royal behest, took a great number of soldiers and ascending a high mountain in the country of Suruga kindled a fire on the summit and there consumed the letter and the deathless medicine,—from which this mountain has been called Fuji-no-Yama, "The Deathless Mountain:" and it is said that the smoke of this fire may still be seen rising towards the clouds.

Translated into English for the
Blessed Children in the far-away
Home Lands by "Uncle Me."

Sometimes the name "Fuji-no-Yama" is written by two characters which mean "rich in soldiers," from the number of soldiers who ascended with the officer to execute the commands of the emperor; and sometimes it is written "no second" because the Princess Splendor will never again visit this earth.

日本昔噺

竹取物語

明治廿二年五月十五日　出　版
明治廿二年五月十四日　印　刷
明治廿二年五月二十日　版權登錄

發行者　東京府平民　長谷川武次郎　東京京橋區丸屋町三

發行所　弘文社　同所

著者　米國人　ミロル　岩手縣稗貫郡大瀨河原七十一番地

畫工　東京府平民　小林永濯　東京府南葛飾郡小梅村三百三十五番地

印刷人　東京府平民　廣瀨安七　東京日本橋區宛町壹番地　製紙分社

www.ingramcontent.com/pod-product-compliance
Lightning Source LLC
Chambersburg PA
CBHW031108020726
47495CB00007B/2101